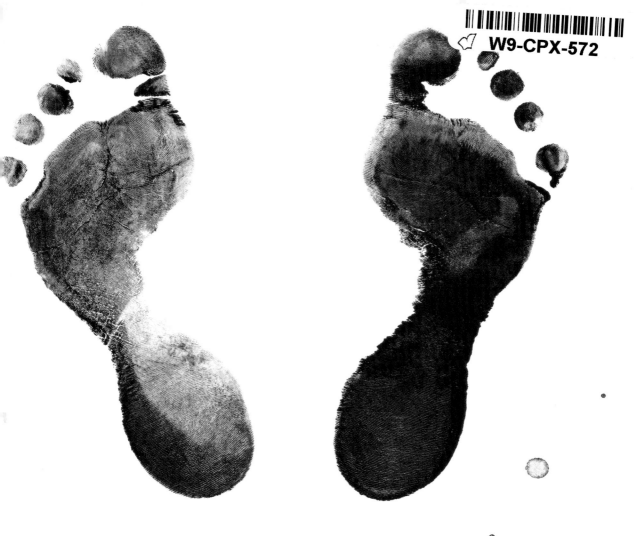

Jake's feet

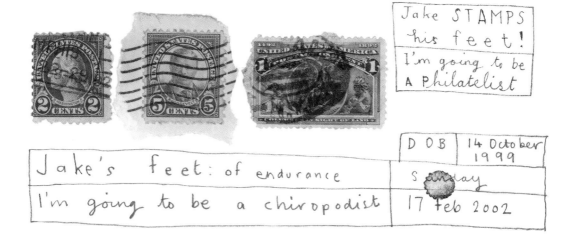

Jake STAMPS his feet!
I'm going to be A Philatelist

Jake's feet: of endurance	DOB	14 October 1999
		Sunday
I'm going to be a chiropodist		17 feb 2002

12 inches = 1 foot
3 feet = 1 yard. → PRACTICE BASKETBALL in your backyard.

1 2 3 4

(HB)

3B   Blue
HB   2B   Red HB   B   (2B)

GROW UP

Sandy Turner

Joanna Cotler Books
An Imprint of HarperCollins
PUBLISHERS

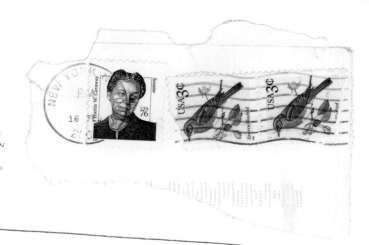

I'M   going to be   GREEN - FINGERED: (a gardener

palm tree?

FOR BILL

and ELEANOR and LYDIA and BLANCHE
not forgetting Jake

WHAT ARE you going TO BE WHEN YOU GROW UP? THE GROWN-UP ASKED THE CHILD.

I don't know,

said the CHILD . . . A NURSE ?

ooh . . . I know
I'm going to be a . . .

SPLASH

I'm going to be a
SCIENTIST

I'm going to be a
DENTIST

I'm going to be a
HYPNOTIST

MOM

I'm going to be a mountain climber

VERY TALL
(EVEN TALLER THAN EVEREST)

EIFFEL TOWER
A FORMER
TALL BUILDING

OR I MIGHT BE

A JOCKEY

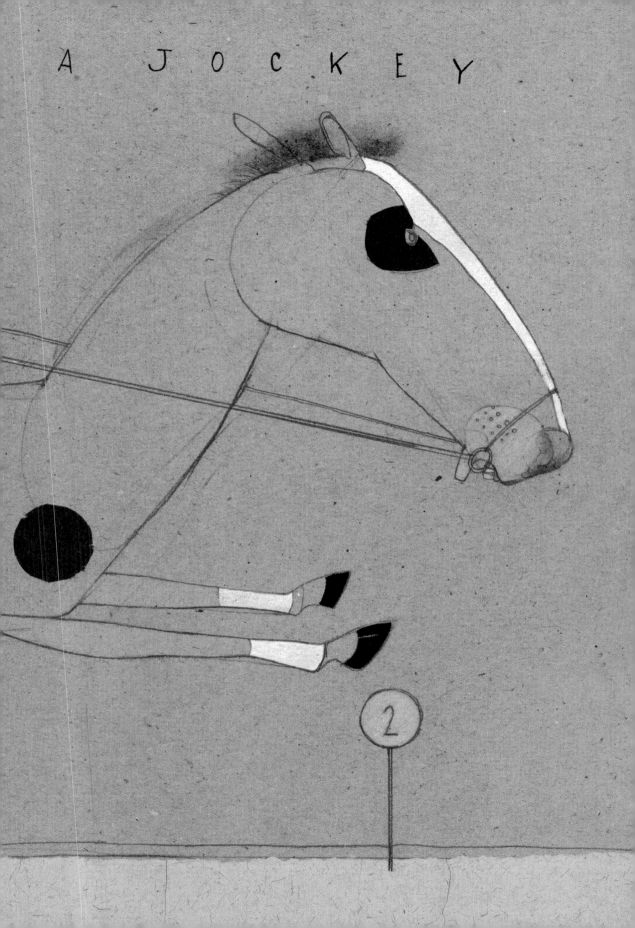

I'M GOING TO BE
A WINDOW CLEANER

AN ASTRONOMER

A MAGICIAN

OR EVEN A LION TAMER

OR A TICKET COLLECTOR

SAXOPHONE

I'm going to play the

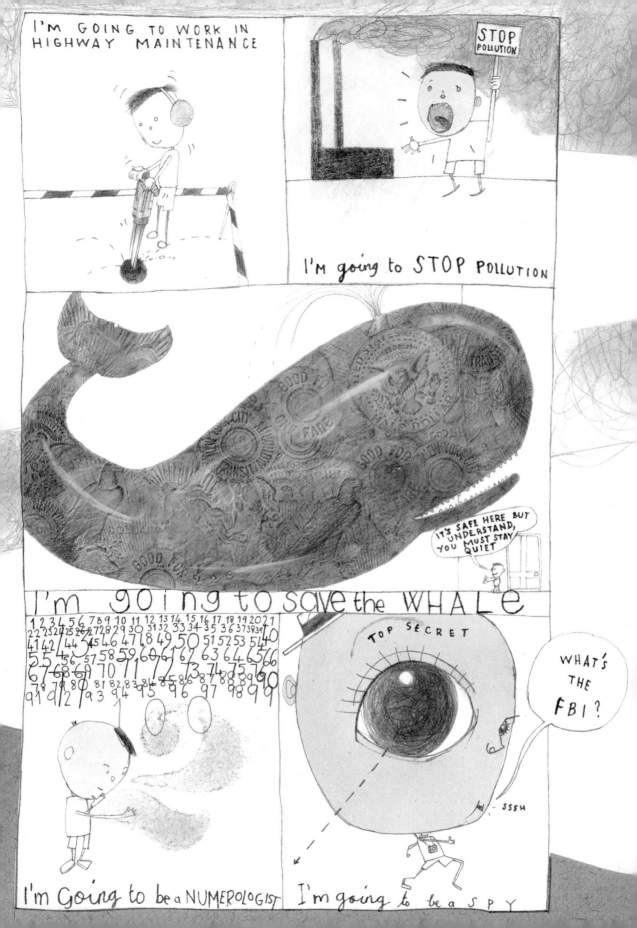

NEW YORK
JUL 19 '01
NY

US POSTAGE
$0.80

LENNY LIGHTHOUSE, esq.
Cape COD
FISHBONE County

I'm going to deliver the U.S. mail.

I Might be a
LIGHTHOUSE
KEEPER

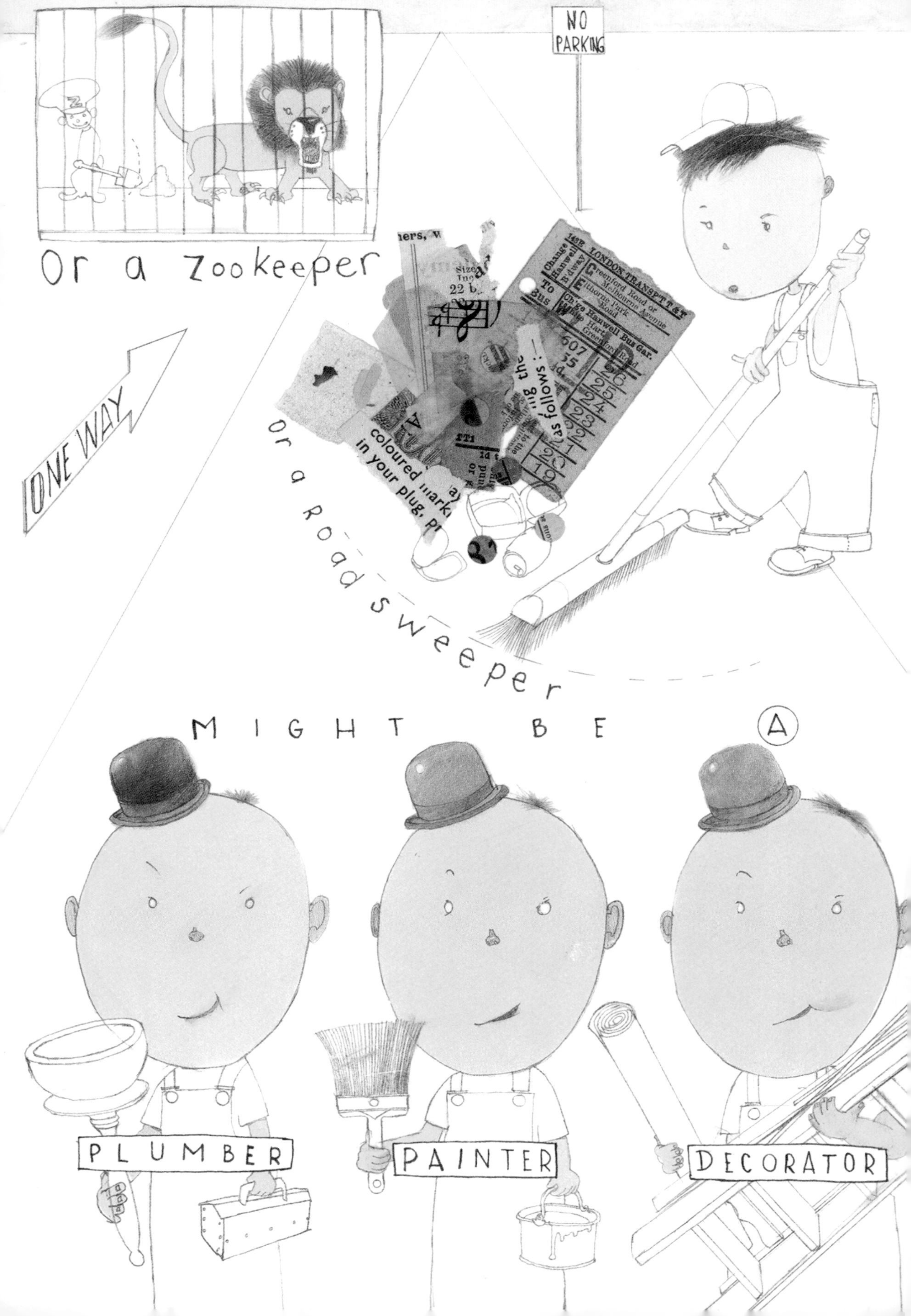

Or a zookeeper

ONE WAY

NO PARKING

Or a road sweeper

MIGHT BE Ⓐ

PLUMBER   PAINTER   DECORATOR

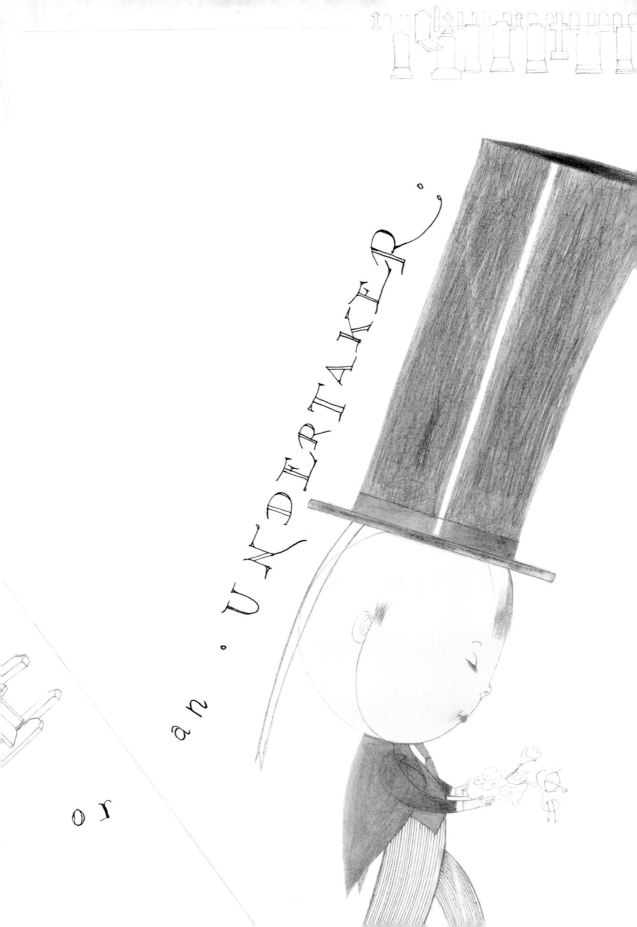

or an · UNDERTAKER.

I might be

Could work on a FERRY: going to be an ARCHITECT: OR I might fly a JET

TO

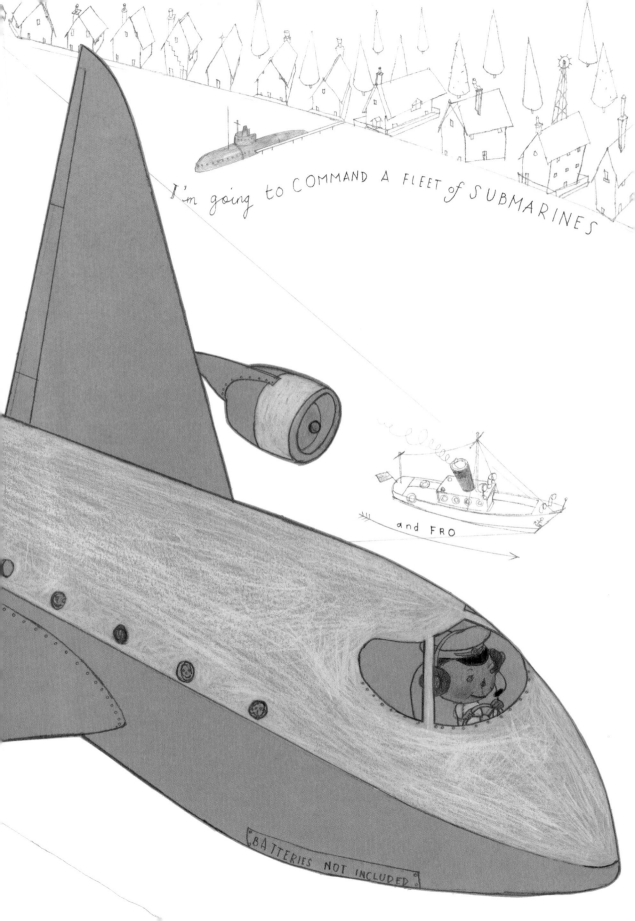

I'm going to COMMAND A FLEET of SUBMARINES

and FRO

BATTERIES NOT INCLUDED

I'm going to grow TALLER

I am going to be the

7' 7"

1

BASKETBALLER.

And the grown-up said

YOU HAD

better

EAT UP

your

GREENS.

How To be an ARTIST:

draw around your hand.

place hand palm side down on the paper. Spread
your fingers evenly. Carefully ~~draw~~ draw round the
edges. Like tracing. Lift your hand away
an' bINGO there is an actual outline of your
HAND.   Add detail, color in.

5

4

3

2

BIG Hand

1

↑

START

older

HANDSome